My Naughty
Little Sister
Stories

When My Naughty Little Sister was Good
My Naughty Little Sister and Bad Harry

Dorothy Edwards
Illustrated by Shirley Hughes

mammoth

First published in Great Britain as two separate volumes:

When My Naughty Little Sister Was Good
Text copyright © 1968 The Estate of Dorothy Edwards
Illustrations copyright © 1968 Shirley Hughes
First published in Great Britain 1968 by Methuen Children's Books Limited
First published in paperback in 1983 by Magnet
This edition first published in 1998 by
Egmont Children's Books Limited
a division of Egmont Holding Limited
239 Kensington High Street, London W8 6SA

My Naughty Little Sister and Bad Harry
Text copyright © 1974 The Estate of Dorothy Edwards
Illustrations copyright © 1974 Shirley Hughes
First published in Great Britain 1974 by Methuen Children's Books Limited
First published in paperback in 1983 by Magnet
This edition first published in 1998 by
Egmont Children's Books Limited
a division of Egmont Holding Limited
239 Kensington High Street, London W8 6SA

This omnibus edition first published in 2000 by Mammoth
an imprint of Egmont Children's Books Limited
a division of Egmont Holding Limited
239 Kensington High Street, London W8 6SA

3 5 7 9 10 8 6 4

ISBN 0 7497 4530 4

Printed and bound in Great Britain by Cox & Wyman Ltd, Reading, Berkshire

Contents

When My Naughty
Little Sister was Good

For Winnie Warne

with love

Contents

1 My Naughty Little Sister learns to talk

Once upon a time, when my sister and I were little children, we had a very nice next-door neighbour called Mrs Jones. Mrs Jones hadn't any children of her own, but she was very fond of my sister and me.

Mrs Jones especially liked my sister. Even when she was naughty! Even when she was a cross and noisy baby with a screamy red face, Mrs Jones would be kind and smily to her, and say, 'There's a duckie, then,' to her.

And sometimes Mrs Jones would be so kind and smily that my bad little sister would forget to scream. She would stare at Mrs Jones instead, and when Mrs Jones said, 'Poor little thing, poor little thing,' to her, my sister would go all mousy quiet for her. My naughty little sister liked Mrs Jones.

When my sister was a very little baby girl, she couldn't talk at all at first. She just made funny, blowy, bubbly noises. But one day, without anyone telling her to, she said, 'Mum, Mum,' to our mother.

We were surprised. We told her she was a very clever baby. And because we were pleased she said, 'Mum, Mum,' again. And again. She said it and said it and said it until we got very used to it indeed.

Then another day, when my sister was saying 'Mum, Mum,' and playing with her piggy toes, she saw our father looking at her, so she said, 'Dad, Dad,' instead!

Father was very excited, and so was Mother, because our funny baby was saying 'Mum, Mum,' and 'Dad, Dad,' as well. I was excited too, and so was dear Mrs Jones.

And because we were so excited my sister went on and on, saying 'Dad, Dad, Dad,' and 'Mum, Mum, Mum,' over and over again until Father, Mother and I weren't a bit excited any more. Only dear Mrs Jones went on being specially pleased about it. She *was* a nice lady!

So, one morning, when Mrs Jones looked over the fence and saw my baby sister in her pram, sucking her finger, she said, 'Don't suck your finger, ducky. Say, "Dad, Dad," and "Mum, Mum," for Mrs Jones.'

And what do you think? My funny sister took her finger out of her mouth and

said 'Doanes'. She said it very loudly, 'DOANES' – like that – and Mrs Jones was so astonished she dropped all her basket of wet washing.

'Doanes, Doanes, Doanes,' my sister

said, because she couldn't quite say 'Jones', and Mrs Jones was so pleased, she left all her wet washing on the path, and ran in to fetch Mr Jones to come and hear.

Mr Jones who had been hammering nails in the kitchen, came out with a hammer in his hand and a nail in his mouth, running as fast as he could to hear my sister say 'Doanes'.

When she said it to him too, Mr Jones said my sister was a 'little knock-out', which meant she was very clever indeed.

After that my sister became their very special friend.

When she got bigger she started to say other words too, but Mr and Mrs Jones still liked it best when she said 'Doanes' to them. If she was in our garden and they were in their garden they always talked to her. Even when she could walk and get into mischief they *still* liked her.

One day a very funny thing happened. Mrs Jones was in her kitchen washing a lettuce for Mr Jones's dinner when she heard a little voice say 'Doanes' and there was my naughty little sister standing on Mrs Jones's back door-step. AND NO ONE WAS WITH HER.

And my little sister was smiling in a very

pleased way.

The back gate was closed and the side gate was closed, and the fence was so high she *couldn't* have got over it.

Mrs Jones was very pleased to see my sister, and gave her a big, big kiss and a jam tart; but she was surprised as well, and said, 'How did you get here, duckie?'

But my little sister still didn't know enough words to tell about things. She just ate her jam tart, then she gave Mrs Jones a big kiss-with-jam-on, but she didn't say anything.

So Mrs Jones took my sister back to our house, and Mrs Jones and Mother wondered and wondered.

The very next day, when Mrs Jones was upstairs making her bed, she heard the little voice downstairs saying, 'Doanes, Doanes!', and there was my sister again!

And the back gate was shut, and the side gate was shut, and the fence was still too high for her to climb over.

Mrs Jones ran straight downstairs, and picked my sister up, and took her home again.

When Mr Jones came home, Mrs Jones told him, and Mother told Father, and they all stood in the gardens and talked. And my sister laughed but she didn't say anything.

Then I remembered something I'd found out when I was only as big as my sister was then. Right up by a big bush at the back of our garden was a place in the fence where the wood wasn't nailed any more, and if you were little enough you could push the wood to the side and get through.

When I showed them the place, everybody laughed. My sister laughed very loud indeed, and then she went through the hole straight away to show how easy it was!

After that, my sister was always going in to see Mrs Jones, but because the hole was so small, and my sister was growing bigger all the time, Mr Jones found another place in his fence, and he made a little gate there.

It was a dear little white gate, with an easy up and down handle. There was a step up to it, and a step down from it. Mr Jones planted a pink rose to go over the top of it, and made a path from the gate to his garden path.

All for my sister. It was her very own gate.

And when Mrs Jones knocked on our wall at eleven o'clock every morning, and my sister went in to have a cup of cocoa with her, she didn't have to go through a hole in the fence, she went through her very own COCOA JONES'S GATE.

2 My Naughty Little Sister's toys

Long ago, when my sister and I were little girls, we had a kind cousin called George who used to like making things with wood.

He made trays and boxes, and things with holes in to hang on the wall for pipes, and when he had made them he gave them away as presents.

George made me a chair for my Teddy-bear and a nice little bookcase for my story-books. Then George thought he would like to make something for my little sister.

Now that wasn't at all easy, because my sister was still a very little child. She still went out in a pram sometimes, she could walk a bit, but when she was in a great hurry she liked crawling better. She could say words though.

My sister had a very smart red pram. She liked her pram very much. She was always pleased when our mother took her out in it.

She learned to say, 'pram, pram, pram,' when she saw it, and 'ride, ride, ride,' to show that she wanted to go out.

Well now, kind Cousin George was sorry to think that my sister liked crawling better than walking, so he said, 'I know, I will make her a little wooden horse-on-wheels so she can push herself along with it.'

And that is just what he did. He made a strong little wooden horse, with a long wavy tail, and a smily-tooth face that he painted himself. He painted the horse white with black spots. Then he put strong red wheels on it, and a strong red handle.

It was a lovely pushing-horse.

I said, 'Oh, isn't it lovely?' and I pushed it up and down to show my sister. 'Look, baby, gee-gee,' I said.

My sister laughed. She was so glad to have the wooden horse. She stood up on her fat little legs and she got hold of the strong red handle, and she pushed too!

And when the horse ran away on his red wheels, my sister walked after him holding on to the red handle, and she walked, and WALKED. Clever Cousin George.

Mother said, 'That's a horse, dear. Say "Thank you, Cousin George, for the nice

horse",' and she lifted my sister up so that she could give him a nice 'thank you' hug, because of course that was the way my sister thanked people in those days.

Then Mother said, 'Horse, horse, horse,' so that my sister could learn the new word, and she patted the wooden horse when she said it.

But my sister didn't say 'Horse' at all. *She* patted the wooden horse too, but she said, 'Pram, pram, pram.'

And she picked up her tiny Teddy-bear, and she laid him on the pushing-horse's back, and she picked up my doll's cot blanket and covered Teddy up with it, and she pushed the horse up and down, and said, 'Pram.'

When George came to see us again, he was surprised to find that my funny little sister had made the horse into a pram, but he said, 'Well, anyway, she can walk now!' And so she could. She had stopped crawling.

Because George liked my little sister he made her another nice thing. He made her a pretty little doll's house, just big enough for her to play with. It had a room upstairs, and a room downstairs, and there were some pretty little chairs and a table and a bed in it that he had made himself.

When my sister saw this doll's house she smiled and smiled. When she opened the front of the doll's house and saw the things inside she smiled a lot more.

She took all the chairs and things out of the doll's house and laid them on the floor, and she began to play with it at once. But she didn't play houses with it at all.

Because there was a room upstairs and a room downstairs and a front that opened she said it was an oven!

She pretended to light a light inside it, just as she had seen our mother do, when she was cooking the dinner, and she said,

'ov-en, ov-en.'

She called the chairs and table and the bed 'Dinner', and she put them back into the doll's house again, and pretended they were cooking, while she took tiny Teddy for a ride on the pushing-horse pram.

She played and played with her doll's house oven and her pushing-horse pram.

Our Cousin George said, 'What an extraordinary child you are.' Then he laughed. 'That gives me an idea!' he said.

And when he went away he was smiling to himself.

The next time George came he was still smiling, and when my sister saw what he had made she smiled too. This time she knew what it was.

George had made a lovely wooden pretending-stove with two ovens and a pretending fire, and a real tin chimney. We don't have stoves like these nowadays, but some people still did when I was young. There was one in our granny's house.

My sister said, 'Gran-gran oven,' at once.

I gave my little sister a toy saucepan and kettle from my toy box, and Mother gave her two little patty-tins.

George said, 'You can cook on the top, and in the ovens – just like Granny does.'

And that was just what my sister did do. She cooked pretending dinners on the wooden stove all day long, and Cousin George was very pleased to think she was playing in the right way with something he had made for her.

But that isn't the end of the story. Oh no.

One day my naughty little sister's bad friend Harry came to visit us with his mother. He was only a little baby boy then, but he liked playing with my sister even in those days.

When my little sister saw Harry, she said, 'Boy-boy. Play oven.' She wanted

Harry to cook dinners too.

Bad Harry looked at the wooden stove, and the real tin chimney and the pretending fire, and he said, 'Engine. Puff-puff.'

Then Harry pretended to put coal into the little fireplace. He opened the oven doors and banged them shut again just like the man who helped the engine-driver did, and he made choof-choof-choofy train noises.

Harry had been with his father to see the trains and he knew just the right noises to make and the right things to do.

My sister didn't know anything about

trains then, but it was such a lovely game that she made all the noises Harry made and said 'Engine' too.

After that she and Harry had lots of lovely games playing engines with the little wooden stove.

When Cousin George heard about this, he said, 'Pram-horses and oven-doll's houses, and now – engine-stoves!'

He said, 'It's no good. When that child is a bigger girl I shall just give her some wood and some nails and let her make her own toys!'

I think he must have forgotten that he said this, because he never did give her any wood and nails. I wonder what she would have made if he had?

3 My Naughty Little Sister and the twins

When my sister was still quite a little child, she liked looking at herself in the looking-glass. She was always asking someone to lift her up so that she could see herself.

She would stare and stare at her funny little self. She made funny faces, and then she would laugh at the funny faces she had made, and then laugh all over again because the little girl in the glass was laughing. She used to amuse herself very much.

When my sister had first seen herself in the mirror she hadn't liked it at all. At first she had been pleased to see the small baby-girl, and had smiled, but when the baby in the glass smiled back, and she put out her hand to touch that baby-girl's smily face – there had only been cold, hard glass. It had been so nasty and so frightening that my poor little sister had cried and cried.

Mother hushed and hushed her and walked up and down with her, and said,

'Don't cry ! Don't cry! It's only you, baby,

it's you in the glass.'

When my sister stopped crying, my mother lifted her up again, and said, 'It's you, baby, in the glass.'

And my sister looked at the poor teary baby in the glass, and she saw that the baby was copying her. She touched the glass again, and the baby touched it too. She got so interested she wasn't frightened any more. She said, 'Baby-in-the-glass!'

So after that, whenever my sister looked at herself in a looking-glass she said, 'Me. Me baby-in-glass.'

When she was neat and nice in a pretty new dress, she said, 'Smart baby-in-glass'. When she saw a dirty little face looking at her she said, 'Dirty baby-in-glass'.

She was a very funny child.

One day we went with our mother to fetch Father's shirts from the Washing Lady's house. Mother did most of our washing, but she sent Father's best shirts to the Washing Lady's house, because she washed them so beautifully and ironed them so cleverly they always looked like new.

Our Washing Lady had a funny little house. Inside her front door there was a room with pictures of ships on the wall, and photographs of sailors on the mantelpiece and seashells on the table.

The sailors were our Washing Lady's sons, and the ships were the ones they sailed the seas in. The Washing Lady was always talking about them.

There was always a steamy smell in the Washing Lady's house, because she was always boiling washing, and an ironing smell because she was always ironing things while the washing was boiling, and there was often a baking smell too, for this kind lady made beautiful curranty biscuits to give to the children who came with their mothers to fetch the washing.

My sister loved to go to the Washing Lady's house.

On the day I'm telling you about, a very funny thing happened when we got to the Washing Lady's house. We knocked at the door as we always did, and then we opened the door as we always did.

Out came a steamy smell and an ironing smell and a baking smell, just as they always did, too.

And then Mother called out, 'May I come in?'

And instead of the Washing Lady standing among the ship and sailor pictures and the seashells, we found two little tiny girls, standing hand in hand; and when they saw our mother and my little sister

and me, they opened their mouths and they both called, 'Grandma, Grandma!'

My little sister stared and stared and stared. She looked at those little girls so much that they both stopped calling and stared back at her.

My sister stared so hard because those tiny little girls were absolutely alike. They had the same little tipping-up noses, the same little twinkly eyes, the same black, curly hair with red ribbons on, the same little blue dresses, the same red socks. *And they had both said 'Grandma' in the same little voices.*

Then the Washing Lady came out from

the back room, and the two little alike girls ran to her, and hung on to her apron.

Mother said, 'These must be your Albert's twinnies then?'

And the Washing Lady said, 'Yes, they are.'

Albert was the Washing Lady's youngest sailor-son. She told Mother that the little girls had come to spend the day with her. She said, 'Albert's boat has come in, and their mother has gone to London to meet him.'

When she said this, the little looking-alike girls smiled again. They said, 'Our daddy is coming home!'

One twinnie said, 'From over the sea –'
The other twinnie said, 'In a big, big boat –'

And the first twinnie said, 'And he's going to bring us –' And the other one said, 'Lots and lots –'

And they both said together, 'Of lovely presents. HOORAY!'

And the funny twinnies fell right down on the floor and kicked their legs in the air to show how happy they were and they laughed and laughed.

My little sister thought they were so funny that she laughed and laughed too, and she fell on the floor and kicked *her* legs in the air. We all laughed then.

Then the Washing Lady told the twinnies to go and fetch the biscuit tin, and they went and fetched it. She gave me a curranty biscuit, and then one to my sister, then she gave one to each of the little twinnies. Then my little sister and the looking-alike girls sat down on the Washing Lady's front step to eat the biscuits, while their Grandma packed up Father's shirts.

When my little sister finished eating her biscuit, she looked very hard at the twins. First at one twin, then at the other twin. Then she put out her hand and touched one little twinny face, and then the other twinny face. She was very quiet, and then she said, 'Which is the looking-glass one?'

That silly little girl thought one twinnie was a real child, and one was a looking-glass child. That was why she touched their faces, and when she couldn't feel any cold, hard glass she was very, very puzzled.

'Which is the looking-glass baby?' she said.

'Good gracious me, what will you ask next?' said our mother. Then she remembered how my sister liked looking at herself in the glass. 'Why,' she said, 'she thinks only one of them is real!'

Our Washing Lady laughed, but she was

a kind lady. She said, 'They are twinnies, dear. Two little girls. There are two looking-glass babies just like them.'

And although she was a very busy lady, she took my little sister and the twinnies upstairs to her bedroom, and showed my sister herself and *two* little looking-alike girls in the wardrobe mirror.

My sister looked at herself in the glass. She looked at the twinnies in the glass. Then she said, 'Thank you very much,' in a funny little voice.

And when we walked home she whispered to me, 'Is there another little real girl like me somewhere?'

I said, 'Oh no, there couldn't be anyone else like you – not anywhere.'

4 The six little Hollidays

Usually, when my sister and I were children, if our mother had to go anywhere special she would take my naughty little sister with her. But if it was somewhere very special indeed she left my sister with Mrs Cocoa Jones next door, or with Bad Harry's mother. Once my sister even spent a day at school with me.

But there was a time once, when Mrs Cocoa was away, and Bad Harry's mother was ill, when my mother didn't quite know what to do about getting my little sister minded.

Mother asked my teacher if my little sister could come to school again, but Teacher said that although she had been such a good child, she wouldn't be able to have her any more because she had minded some other little sisters in the school who hadn't been good at all. They had been so fidgety and naughty that she had had to say, no more minding!

The teacher said, 'I am afraid they are

not all good like your little girl.'

Just fancy that!

Well, my mother was very anxious about my sister, because she knew my sister could be very shy with people. She couldn't think of anyone who might want to mind a shy, cross girl for a whole afternoon.

When she was coming back from the school, she met a lady she knew and told her all about it. The lady was called Mrs Holliday, and Mrs Holliday said at once, 'Oh, don't worry about that. We will mind her with pleasure. We will call round for her at two o'clock.'

My mother was very glad that Mrs Holliday was going to mind my sister, although she couldn't help wondering if my sister would behave herself.

When our mother told my sister that she was going to spend an afternoon with Mrs Holliday my sister looked very cross and frightened. She stuck her lip out and her face went red as red, and our mother said, 'Oh dear, don't be awkward, will you?'

I think my sister *would* have been awkward. She might have bellowed and shouted, but just then there was a knock on our back door and there stood Mrs Holliday herself, all ready and smiling, and behind Mrs Holliday, looking as shy and peepy as my little sister herself, were five little children: three little boys and two little girls.

Right up at the end of our garden by the back gate stood a very tall, very wide sort of perambulator-pushchair, and peeping out from under the hood of that was another little child!

My sister *did* stare, and all the little Hollidays stared. Mrs Holliday was a lady with red, rosy cheeks, and all the children had red, rosy cheeks too. And although they all wore different coloured coats and scarves they all wore bright blue woolly hats.

'We won't come in,' Mrs Holliday said, 'because our shoes are muddy.'

When my sister was ready, Mrs Holliday said, 'Come along, dear, don't take any notice of my children. They are all *very shy*, but they will talk nineteen to the dozen as soon as they are used to you.'

My sister was a shy child, but she had never seen so many shy children together before, and she quite forgot her own shyness when she saw them all hiding behind their mother.

Our mother said she hoped Mrs Holliday wouldn't find my sister too much for her, but Mrs Holliday said, 'One more will hardly be noticed.'

Then Mrs Holliday called the children out from behind her and said, 'These boys are John and David, and they are twins. This is Jean, and this is Susan, and they are twins too. The big boy Tom, he has a bad arm, so he is not at school today, and the baby is Billy.'

Then Mrs Holliday told Jean and Susan to take my little sister's hands, and off they all went, all shy and quiet and peepy, down the garden to the back gate and the big perambulator-pushchair.

There sat baby Billy with his legs dangling down under a shiny black cover

like a pram cover. He was peeping out from under a big black hood like a pram hood. There was a handle behind the hood like a pushchair handle.

My sister was so surprised to see this funny pram-pushchair, she said, 'That's a funny thing.'

When my sister said this, all the little Hollidays laughed together, and stopped being shy, because they thought it was a funny thing too, and then they waited for their mother to tell my little sister all about it.

Mrs Holliday said, 'It's a very special chair, this is. It was once used by FOREIGN ROYALTY.' And she looked so pleased and so proud when she said this, that my sister knew it must be something very grand.

Mrs Holliday said, 'It was specially made for Royal Twins – that is why it is so wide; and although it's nearly fifty years old, it's still as good as new.'

Mrs Holliday said that as my sister was a visitor, she could ride with Billy in the royal pushchair, and my sister was so pleased she could hardly remember to say 'good-bye' to our mother.

Off they went down the street, Mrs Holliday behind the perambulator-pushchair with little Hollidays on either side, and my little sister very smiling and pleased and not shy, with Billy beside her. Billy was a dear little baby boy, and when he saw my sister was smiling and pleased, he was smiling and pleased too. They looked very happy children.

As they went along everybody they met

smiled to see the funny pram-pushchair and the rosy Hollidays with their blue woolly hats and my happy little sister.

Mrs Holliday took them through the park, and they went a way my sister hadn't been before, so it was very interesting. In the park my sister got out of the pram-pushchair and ran and scuffled in the leaves with the other children. The leaves lay all over the paths, red and yellow and brown, and all the little Hollidays shouted with excitement and my sister shouted too.

When Mrs Holliday thought they had played enough they went off again. This time one of the little girl twins rode with

Billy, and my little sister ran through the park with the other children. It was fun!

Outside the park, Tom, who had the bad arm, said, 'Before we go home we are going to the baker's, aren't we, Mother?'

And all the other little Hollidays shouted, 'Yes. Yes. For cookie-boys.'

They were all very excited, so my sister got excited too and they went down a street and stopped outside a funny little baker's shop.

Mrs Holliday said that as my sister hadn't been there before she could come in with her. All the Holliday children stood outside and pushed their faces against the window to watch.

Inside the shop was a dear old lady, and when she saw Mrs Holliday she said, 'I know what you have come for: six cookie-boys.'

But Mrs Holliday said, 'Not six. *Seven* today. I've got an extra little child, who has never had one of your cookie-boys before.'

The old lady said, 'Then I must find her a very nice one.'

She took down a big wooden tray, and in it there lay dozens and dozens of shiny brown cookie-boys.

Do you know what cookie-boys are? They are buns made in the shape of funny little men, with currant eyes and noses and mouths and rows of currants all down their fronts for buttons!

The old lady's cookie-boys were the shiniest and the stickiest cookie-boys ever made, and people came a long way to buy them.

The old lady put six cookie-boys in a bag for Mrs Holliday, and then she chose a special one and put it in a special bag for my little sister.

When they got

to Mrs Holliday's house, they all sat round a big table and had tea and bread-and-butter and jam, and when they had eaten and eaten, they finished off with their cookie-boys.

My sister had just finished eating hers when our mother came to fetch her.

And what do you think? When she saw my mother, my sister began to cry and cry. She said, 'I don't want to go home yet.'

Our mother was very surprised.

But Mrs Holliday said, 'Now, be a good girl, and you shall come another day.'

And my sister stopped crying at once. And she did visit them again, too.

5 The bonfire pudding

When my sister was a little girl she didn't like Bonfire Night and fireworks. She didn't like them at all. I liked them very much and so did my sister's friend Harry, but she didn't.

She wouldn't even look out of the window on Bonfire Night.

She would say, 'It's burny and bangy, and I don't like it.'

So on Bonfire Nights, Mother stayed home with her, while our father took me out to let the fireworks off.

It was a pity because our mother *did* like fireworks.

Well now, one day, just before the Fifth of November (which is what Bonfire Night day is called) our mother took us round to our grandmother's house to pay a visit, and Mother told Grannie all about my little sister not liking fireworks.

She said, 'It's such a pity, because this year the fireworks are going to be very grand. There is going to be a big bonfire on the common, and everyone is going there to let off fireworks.'

She said, 'There is going to be a Grand Opening with the Mayor, and a Band on a Lorry.'

Our mother said, 'I am sure she would like it. She likes music.'

But my sister looked very cross. She said, 'I do like music very much. But I don't like fireworks.'

Mother said, 'But they are going to have baked potatoes and sausages and spicy cakes and all sorts of nice things to eat.'

My sister said, 'I don't like bonfires.'

Mother said, 'You see, she is a stubborn

child. She won't try to like them.'

But our grannie wasn't a bit surprised. She said, 'Well, I don't like bonfires or fireworks either. I never did. I was always glad to get my children out of the house on the Fifth of November. It gave me a chance to do something much more interesting.'

My little sister was glad to know that our grandmother didn't like fireworks either, so she went right up to Grannie's chair and held her hand.

Grannie said, 'You don't like fireworks and no more do I. Why don't you come and visit me on Firework Night? I think I can find something interesting for you to do.'

When Grannie said this, she shut one of her eyes up, and made a funny face at my sister. She said, 'Why don't you come and have some fun with me? Then your mother can go to the common with your daddy and sister and have fun too.'

My sister made a funny face back at Grannie, and said, 'Yes, I think I should like that.'

So on Bonfire Night, before it got too dark, Mother wrapped my little sister up in a warm coat and a big shawl and put her in a pushchair and hurried round to Grandmother's house.

She left my sister as soon as Grannie

opened the door, because she was in a hurry to get back.

'Come in,' said Grannie to my little sister. 'You are just in time.' She helped my sister take her things off, and then she said, 'Now, into the kitchen, Missy.'

It was lovely and warm in the kitchen in our grannie's house. My sister was very pleased to see the big fire and the black pussy asleep in front of it.

'Look,' said Grannie. 'It's all ready.'

Grannie's big kitchen table looked just like a shop, there were so many things on it. There were jars and bottles and packets, full of currants and sultanas and raisins and ginger and candied peel and a big heap of suet on a board, and a big heap of brown sugar on a plate. There were apples and oranges and lemons, and even some big clean carrots!

There was a big brown bowl standing on a chair that had a big, big, wooden spoon in it. And on the draining board were lots of white basins.

Can you guess? My sister couldn't. She didn't know what all this stuff was for, so Grannie said, 'We are going to make the Family Christmas Puddings. I always make one for every one of my children every year. And I always make them on Bonfire

night. IT TAKES MY MIND OFF THE
BANGS.'

My sister was very surprised to hear
this, and to know that all these lovely
things to eat were going to be made into
Christmas Puddings.

Grannie said, 'You can help me, and it
will take your mind off the bangs, too.'

She said, 'I've looked out a little apron;
it will just fit you. It used to belong to one
of your aunties when she was a little girl.'

And she tied a nice white apron round
my sister's little middle.

'Now,' Grannie said, 'climb up to the
sink, and wash and scrub your hands. They

must be clean for cookery.'

So my sister climbed up to the sink and washed her hands, and Grannie dried them for her, and then she was ready to help.

Grannie found lots of things for her to do, and they laughed all the time.

Grannie was quick as quick, and every time my sister finished doing one thing, she found something else for her to do at once.

Grannie poured all the currants out on to the table and my sister looked to see if there were any stalky bits left in them. When she had done that, Grannie told her to take the almonds out of the water, and pop them out of their brown skins. That was a lovely thing to do. When my sister popped an almond into her mouth Grannie only laughed and said, 'I'll have one as well.'

Grannie chopped the suet, then the almonds, and the ginger while my sister put the currants and sultanas and things into the big brown bowl for her. It was quite a hard job because she had to climb up and down so much, but she did it, and she didn't spill anything either. Grannie was pleased.

Grandmother chopped the candied peel, and because my sister was so good and helpful she gave her one of the lovely, sugary, candied peel middles to suck.

While Grannie crumbled bread and chopped apples and carrots, she let my sister press the oranges and lemons in the squeezer.

All the time they chattered and laughed and never thought about Bonfire Night. They never noticed the bangs.

Once the black pussy jumped out of the chair and ran and hid himself under the dresser, but they were laughing so much they didn't even notice.

At the very end, Grannie broke a lot of eggs into a basin; then she held the mixer while my sister turned the handle to beat them up.

And sometimes, while they were working, Grannie would make a funny face at my sister, and eat a sultana, and sometimes my sister would make a funny face at Grannie and eat a raisin!

When all the things had been put into the brown bowl, Grannie began to mix and mix with the big spoon. She gave my sister a little wooden spoon so that she could mix too.

Then, Grannie said, 'Now you must shut your eyes and stir, and make a wish. You always wish on a Christmas pudding mixture.'

And my sister did. She shut her eyes and turned her spoon round and round. Then Grannie shut her eyes and wished.

My sister said, 'I wished I could come and help you next Bonfire night, Grannie.'

And Grannie said, 'Well, Missy, that was just what I wished too!'

Then my sister sat quietly by the fire while our grandmother put the pudding mixture into all the basins, and covered them with paper and tied them with cloth.

My sister was very tired now, but she sat smiling and watching until Father came to fetch her.

Our Father said, 'Goodness, Mother, do you still make the Christmas Puddings on Bonfire Night? Why, you used to when I was a boy.'

Grannie said, 'This little girl and I think Bonfire Night is the best time of all for making Christmas puddings.'

She said, 'You may as well take your pudding now. It must be boiled all day tomorrow and again on Christmas Day. It should be extra good this year, as I had such a fine helper!'

So Father brought it home that night and on Christmas Day we had it for dinner.

My sister was so proud when she saw it

going into the water on Christmas morning she almost forgot her new toys.

And when we were sitting round the table, and Father poured brandy on it, and lit it, so that the pudding was covered with little blue flames, my sister said, 'Now it's a real bonfire pudding.'

6 Harry's shouting coat

Long ago, when my sister was a funny little girl with a friend called Harry, Harry had an auntie who lived over the sea in Canada, and this auntie used to send Harry presents.

Sometimes she sent him toys, sometimes she sent him sweeties. But once she sent him a very bright coat.

It was the loveliest coat Harry had ever

seen. It was the loveliest coat my little sister had ever seen.

It was bright, bright red, and it had a bright, bright yellow collar and bright, bright yellow pockets and shiny goldy buttons and there was white twisty cord round the buttons.

My sister was playing at Harry's house when the coat-parcel came, and they were both very excited.

Harry tried the coat on at once, and walked up and down to show my sister, and then my sister tried it on and walked up and down to show Harry.

But do you know, Harry's mother didn't

like that coat at all! She said, 'I really don't think you can wear it to go out in. It's far too loud.'

When she showed the coat to Harry's father, he said, 'Yes, it's loud all right. It shouts.'

Harry's father and mother laughed then. But Harry didn't laugh and my sister didn't laugh. Harry was thoroughly cross. He said, 'It's a very nice coat. Auntie sent it for me. I want to wear it.'

His father said, 'Well, you can wear it in the garden and frighten the birds with it. Then they won't eat all the seeds.'

But Harry didn't want to wear that

beautiful coat in the garden. He wanted to wear it where all the other children could see it. My sister wanted him to wear it where all the other children could see it too. She wanted to be with him when everyone was looking at his smart red coat.

She said, 'I think it's a beautiful coat, Harry.'

Harry said, 'I want to wear it outside.' Harry was very cross when he said, 'I want to wear it,' but he didn't shout. He had a little, little cross voice.

Harry had a shouting voice too. He used to shout at my naughty little sister sometimes, but he had a little, cross voice too.

Harry's mother didn't like to be unkind about the red coat because after all it was Harry's present, so she had a good idea. She said, 'All right, you can wear it out one day if you are a *very good boy*.'

She said this because she thought Harry wouldn't be good.

But he was.

Those two naughty children went out into the garden, and whispered and whispered and they made up their minds that Harry would be good, and he was!

My sister helped him to be good. She didn't quarrel with him or grumble at him. She was good and polite to him, and Harry

was good and polite to her. Do you know how they managed it? They played a game of being good and polite people. It was fun!

When Harry was at home he was still good. He helped his father and tidied up his toys, and he kept saying to his mother, 'Haven't I been good enough yet?' Until at last she said Harry could wear his coat tomorrow.

She said she would take Harry and my sister for a picnic on the Island and Harry could wear his red coat.

Harry and my sister were very pleased about this, because they liked going to the Island very much.

The Island was in the middle of the river. There was an old man in a sailor hat and a blue coat to row you in a boat to the Island, and to come and fetch you later on. He was the ferryman.

It was lovely to sit in the boat with the water all around you. You had to sit very still on the seats or the old man shouted at you. So you couldn't play anything, but it was still very nice.

Sometimes there were lots of people going to the Island, but on this picnic day when Harry wore his loud red coat, there was only Harry's mother, and Harry and my little sister.

The old ferryman wasn't there either. There was just a boy to row the boat. The boy said the old man was his grandad. He said his grandad had gone to get some new teeth, but he would be back later on.

Harry and my sister were disappointed there were no other people going to the Island; they wanted to show off the coat. Lots of people had stared when they went through the town, and they had been very proud. A postman had said, 'My, my!' and a boy had whistled, and some people had come out of a shop to look. It had been exciting.

Harry's mother said she wasn't sorry no one else was going to the Island.

Although there were no other people, Harry and my sister had a lovely time. They ran all round the Island first. Then they played house-on-fire. My sister sat under a bush that was the house, and Harry was the fire-engine and the fireman too in his red coat and shiny buttons.

Then they ate their picnic, and Harry's mother said she would have a little nap before the ferryman came to fetch them. Harry said he would have a nap too, because he had got hot and tired running about in his coat all the time, and my sister said she would have a nap as well as there wouldn't be anyone to play with, so she lay down too, and soon everyone was fast asleep.

Harry's mother woke up first of all, and when she woke up she was very worried. She woke Harry and my sister up, and they were very cross and sleepy at first.

She said, 'Oh, do wake up properly, children. It's late and the boat hasn't come.'

They all ran to look across the river then, and Harry and my sister forgot to be sleepy because Harry's mother was so worried.

They saw the boat tied up across the river, but there was no boat boy and no old ferryman.

Harry's mother said, 'Oh dear, they have

forgotten us!'

When she said this, my sister started to cry, because it sounded so nasty to be forgotten, and then Harry cried too, and his mother had to make a fuss of them until they stopped.

'Never mind,' she said. 'We will wait, and when we see anyone we will call out, and they will know we are here.'

They waited and waited, and, just as they were beginning to think they might have to sleep on the Island all night, they saw the old man in his sailor hat coming down the path by the boat.

They shouted and shouted. But the old man took no notice. They shouted again,

but he didn't hear them.

He looked across. He stood still, then he waved and waved to them. He untied the boat, got in it, and began to row and row, straight to the Island.

They were glad to see him.

When he rowed them back, he told Harry's mother that his grandson had forgotten to tell him about them. He said, 'I was just coming to put the boat away.'

Harry's mother said, 'It's a good thing we shouted, then.'

But the old man said, 'I didn't hear any shouting, Mam. I didn't hear anything.'

He said, 'If I hadn't looked across and

seen this young chap's coat, I shouldn't have known anyone was here.'

When the old man said this, Harry looked at my little sister and she looked at him. 'Father said the coat shouted,' Harry said.

'It's a good thing it was *loud*,' said my sister. 'I don't think I would like to sleep on the Island very much.'

When they got home again, Harry's mother said, 'Well, at least you won't get lost in that coat. It's too conspicuous. I think you had better wear it when we go to the park or one of the other places you sometimes get lost in.'

And that is just what Harry did. Sometimes, when they played in the park, he let my sister borrow it for a treat, so that she could run about in the bracken without getting lost.

7 The baby angel

When I was a little girl, and my sister was a little girl, our dear next-door friend Mrs Cocoa Jones was always washing and dusting and polishing her clean, tidy house.

My little sister often went to visit Mrs Jones when she was doing her work. Sometimes she helped her, and sometimes she just sat and watched.

Mr Cocoa Jones was always busy too. He painted and sawed and nailed and glued things. He stuck up wallpaper and mended pipes. When he wasn't doing these things he would go outside and do something new to his garden.

He didn't just plant flowers and vegetables like our father. Oh no! He made pretty paths with big stones, and stuck seashells like fans all along the edges. He put a big stone basin on top of a pipe for the birds to bath in, and he made a garden seat for Mrs Cocoa out of twisty branches. My sister used to love watching clever Mr Jones at work.

One day Mr Jones brought home a big barrowful of rocks and stones. He put all these stones in a heap by his back door. Then he put lots of earth on the heap, and planted flowers in the earth.

My sister said, 'What are you doing that for, Mr Cocoa?' and Mr Cocoa said he was making a rockery. He said in the summer, when the flowers were out, it would make a nice bit of colour.

And when the summer came Mr Cocoa's rockery was very beautiful. It was so beautiful that Mother said she would like a rockery too, and Father said he would make one for her next spring.

My sister said she would like a rockery as well, but she didn't wait at all. She went down to the rubbishy end of our garden, and collected lots of bricks and stones and earth and made herself a little rockery right away.

My funny sister made her rockery, but she didn't put flowers on it like Mr Cocoa did. She looked all over our rubbish heap and found pieces of blue glass and red glass and broken china with pretty patterns on it, and she stuck them on her rockery instead.

Mr Cocoa said my sister's rockery was a good idea, because it would be pretty all year round. He said his rockery was only pretty when the flowers were out.

My little sister smiled a lot then, and kind Mr Cocoa said if she wanted any more things for her rockery she could come and look at his rubbish heap, and see if she could find anything. 'Only mind you don't cut yourself on something sharp,' Mr Cocoa said, 'or I'll have Mrs Jones after me!'

My sister found a lot of interesting things for her rockery on the Cocoa Jones's rubbish heap. She found pieces of china and glass, and a piece of an old bubble-pipe. She found one of those diamond-looking, sparkly bottle stoppers, and one of

Mr Cocoa's path shells that he had thrown away because he didn't need it. She found half a little crockery dog, and a *round white china thing*, with a pretty little china face on it.

My sister was very pleased with all these things, and she put them on her rockery as well. She put the little half-dog on the top, and the pretty smiling-face thing in front where it smiled and smiled. Everybody said her rockery looked very pretty. Even Father, and he didn't often say things like that.

Well now, one day when my sister went to visit Mrs Cocoa, she found that dear lady very busy. Mrs Cocoa had a very beautiful best front-room, and in this room was a big glass cupboard with all Mrs Cocoa's very best china in it.

When my sister came in, Mrs Cocoa was washing all her lovely china from the glass cupboard, and she said, if my sister would promise not to touch anything, she could come and stand on the stool by the table and watch her.

Mrs Jones had lots of lovely china, and she washed it all very carefully in soapy water, and dried it very, very carefully on an old soft towel. She had plates with roses on, and teapots and vases and little

Chinamen, and ladies with fans, and dishes, and tiny red drinking glasses. My sister hadn't seen all these things close to before, but she only looked; she didn't touch a thing!

When Mrs Cocoa was washing a black teapot with yellow daises on it, she said, 'Oh dear! There's something in here!'

My sister looked to see what was in the teapot, and Mrs Jones showed her a wet, soapy paper bundle.

'Oh dear,' said Mrs Cocoa. 'I'd forgotten about the baby angel.'

And she carefully opened the wet soapy paper, and inside was a white china baby angel with tiny wings and no clothes on. It was holding a white china basket with white flowers in it.

My sister looked hard at the little angel. She said, 'Oh, poor, poor angel. It hasn't got a head!' And it hadn't.

Mrs Cocoa said, 'All this china came from my old auntie's. The little angel was broken when we unpacked it, but Mr Jones said he would mend it for me.'

Then she told my sister that Mr Cocoa hadn't been able to mend it because the head had disappeared.

Mrs Cocoa said, 'I suppose it must have got burned up when Mr Jones got rid of all the paper the china was wrapped in. It's such a shame. I always loved that little angel when I was a girl!'

My sister looked hard at that baby angel, and then she remembered something. She remembered the round china white thing with the pretty smiling face that she had put on her rockery.

She didn't say a word to Mrs Cocoa. She slipped off the stool, and ran out of the house, through her own little gate, up our garden, straight to her rockery and back again.

'Here it is, Mrs Cocoa. Here it is,' my sister said. 'Here's the baby angel's head. It was on my rockery.'

Mrs Cocoa Jones was delighted. She ran in to tell Mother about my sister's cleverness in finding the baby angel's little head. She told Mr Jones when he came home, and he got out his sticky glue and stuck it on at once. It looked very pretty when it was mended.

Mrs Cocoa took the baby angel in to show my sister, and my sister saw that it was smiling at the basket of white flowers.

'You are a good, clever child!' Mrs Cocoa said. She said that if my sister hadn't been so clever and made such a lovely rockery she would never have found the angel's head. She said it must have fallen out of the paper when Mr Cocoa burned the rubbish many years ago.

Mrs Cocoa said, 'I prize that little angel very much.' But she said that when my sister was a lady of twenty-one she would give her the baby angel for her very own! Wasn't that kind of her?

She did too, and if you go to my good, grown-up sister's house you will see the baby angel smiling at his flowers on my sister's mantelpiece.

My Naughty Little Sister
and Bad Harry

For Martine and

Olivia Jane Edwards

with love

Contents

1 My Naughty Little Sister and Bad Harry

Once upon a time – a long time ago – when I was a little girl, I had a sister who was littler than me. Now although my sister was sometimes very naughty she had a lot of friends. Some of her friends were grown-up people but some were quite young. Her favourite child-friend was a little boy called Harry. He often made my sister cross so she called him Bad Harry.

Bad Harry lived quite near to us. There were no roads to cross to get to his house, and he and my sister often went round to visit each other without any grown-up person having to take them.

One day, when my naughty little sister went round to Bad Harry's house it was his mother's washing day. Bad Harry was very pleased to see her; he didn't like it when his mother was doing washing.

'Have you come to play?' he asked.

Now Harry's mother didn't like naughty children running about in her house while she was doing the washing, so she said, 'You'll have to play in the garden then. You know what you two are like when there's water about!'

Harry said he didn't mind that. There was

a lovely game they could play in the garden.
They could play *Islands*.

There was a big heap of sand at the
bottom of the garden that Harry's father was
going to make a path with one day. Harry
said, 'We'll pretend that sand is an island in
the river, like the one we go to on the ferry-
boat sometimes.'

My sister said, 'Yes. We will go and live on it. We will say that all the garden is the river.'

So off they went.

They had a good game pretending to live on the island. They filled Harry's toy truck with sand and ran it up and down the heap and tipped the sand over the island's side until it became quite flat.

Then they dug holes in the sand and stuck sticks in them and said they were planting trees.

Later on Harry went to find some more sticks and while he was gone my sister made sand-pies for their pretending dinner. My little sister made them in a flower-pot and tipped them out very carefully. They did look nice.

'Dinner time, Harry,' she said.

But instead of pretending to eat a sand pie, that bad Bad Harry knocked all the pies over with a stick.

He said, 'Now you will have to make some more.'

He thought that was a funny thing to do. But my sister didn't think so.

My naughty little sister was very, very cross with Bad Harry when he knocked her pies over. She screamed and shouted and said, 'Get off my island, bad, Bad Harry,' and she pushed him and he fell on to the garden.

When Harry fell my sister stopped being cross. She laughed instead. 'Now you're all wet in the river,' she said.

But Bad Harry didn't laugh. He was very angry.

'I'm not wet. I'm not wet,' he shouted, and he began to jump up and down. 'You pushed me. You pushed me,' Harry said.

'You broke my pies,' shouted my sister, 'Bad old Harry,' and *she* jumped up and down too.

Bad Harry was just going to shout again when he saw something and had an idea: he saw his mother's washing-basket.

Harry's mother had filled the washing-line with sheets and she'd left the other wet things in a basket on the path so that she could hang them up when the sheets were dry.

'I've got a boat,' Harry said.

He went up to the basket with the wet things in it.

'Look,' he said. 'It's a boat!' And he began to push it along the path.

My sister forgot about being cross with Harry because she liked his idea so much. She went to help him push.

'We've got a boat,' she said.

They pushed their boat round and round the island, and they were just talking about giving each other rides in it, on top of the wet washing, and my sister was just shouting again because she wanted to be first, when Harry's mother came out.

'You are naughty children,' Harry's mother said. 'If I hadn't caught you in time you would have got all my washing dirty. What will you do next?'

'We were playing Islands,' Bad Harry said.

'Well, you are not going to play Islands any more,' said Harry's mother. 'You will come indoors with me where I can keep an eye on you!'

'Now,' she said. 'You can each sit on a chair while I wash the kitchen floor.'

She lifted Bad Harry on to one chair, and my naughty little sister on to another chair, and she said, 'Don't you *dare* get off!'

And they *didn't* dare get off. Harry's mother looked too cross. They didn't even talk – they were so busy watching her washing the floor.

First she used the mop on one corner. Then she picked up the chair with Bad Harry on it and put it on the wet place.

'There!' she said.

Then she washed the floor in another corner. She picked up the chair with my naughty little sister on it and put it on that wet place.

'There!' she said. 'Now don't get down till the floor is dry!'

She said, 'Curl your feet up and keep them out of the wet.'

And Bad Harry curled his feet, and my little sister curled her feet, and Bad Harry's mother laughed and said, 'Right, here I go!'

And she mopped all the floor that was left. She did it very, very quickly.

My little sister quite enjoyed watching Harry's mother mop the floor. She liked to see the mop going round and round and all the soap bubbles going round and round too. She liked to see it going backwards and forwards wiping up the bubbles. Every time the bubbles were wiped up she shouted, 'Gone away!' Our mother didn't clean *her* floor like that – so it was very interesting.

Bad Harry didn't shout though. He went very still and very quiet. He was thinking.

When Harry's mother was finished, she said, '*Well*, you *have* been good children. I'll just put some newspaper over the floor and you can get down.'

So she put newspaper all over the floor, and my little sister got down off her chair.

'Let's go and find a chocolate biscuit,' Harry's kind mother said.

My little sister smiled because she liked chocolate biscuits, but Bad Harry didn't smile. He didn't get down from his chair. He was still thinking.

He was pretending. All the time he had been on the chair he had been playing Islands. He had been pretending that the chair was an island and the wet floor was a river.

'Come on, Harry,' my naughty little sister said. 'Come and get your biscuit.'

'I can't. I'll fall in the river,' said Harry. 'I can't swim yet.'

My little sister knew at once that Harry had been playing. She looked at the wet floor with the paper all over it, then she pulled the paper across the floor and laid it in a line from Harry's chair to the door. 'Come over the bridge,' she said.

And that's what he did. And after that they made up all sorts of games with newspapers on the floor.

2 The icy cold tortoise

Long ago, when I was a little girl and had a little sister, we lived next door to a kind lady called Mrs Jones. My sister used to call this lady Mrs Cocoa sometimes.

If my mother had to go out and couldn't take my little sister this kind next-door lady used to mind her. My sister was always glad to be minded by dear Mrs Jones and Mrs Cocoa Jones was always glad to mind my little sister. They enjoyed minding days very much.

Well now, one cold blowy day when the wind was pulling all the old leaves off the trees to make room for the new baby ones to grow, our mother asked Mrs Cocoa Jones to mind my sister while she went shopping.

Mrs Cocoa and my sister had a lovely time. They swept up all the leaves from Mr Jones's nice tidy paths and put them into a heap for him to burn. They went indoors and laid Mr Jones's tea, and they were just going to sit down by the fire to have a rest when they heard Mr Cocoa coming down the back path.

Mr Cocoa came down the path pushing his bicycle with one hand and holding a very strange-looking wooden box with holes in it in the other hand.

When Mr Jones saw my little sister

peeping at him out of his kitchen window he smiled and smiled. 'Hello, Mrs Pickle,' he said. 'What are you doing here, then?'

'I'm being minded,' said my little sister. Then, because she was an inquisitive child she said, 'What have you got in that box, Mr Cocoa?'

'Just wait a minute, and I'll show you,' Mr Cocoa said, and he went off to put his bicycle in the shed.

'I wonder what's in that box, Mrs Cocoa?' said my inquisitive little sister.

'It's a very funny box – it's got holes in it.'

'Ah,' said Mrs Cocoa, 'just you wait and see!'

When kind Mr Cocoa came in and saw my impatient little sister he was so good he didn't even stop to take off his coat. He

opened the box at *once* – and he showed my sister an icy-cold tortoise, lying fast asleep under a lot of hay.

Have you ever seen a tortoise? My little sister hadn't.

Tortoises are very strange animals. They have hard round shells and long crinkly necks and little beaky noses. They have tiny black eyes and four scratchy-looking claws.

But when they are asleep you can't see their heads or their claws; they are tucked away under their shells. They just look like cold round stones.

My little sister thought the tortoise was a stone at first. She touched it, and it was icy-cold. 'What is it?' she said. 'What is this stone-thing?'

Mr Cocoa picked the tortoise up and

showed her where the little claws were tucked away, and the beaky little shut-eyed face under the shell.

'It's a tortoise,' Mr Cocoa said.

'He's having his winter sleep now,' said Mrs Cocoa.

Mr Jones told my sister that one of the men who worked with him had given him the tortoise, because he was going away and wouldn't have anywhere to keep it in his new home.

'I shall put him away in the cupboard under the stairs now,' he said. 'He will sleep there all the winter and wake up again when the warm days come.'

Just as Mr Cocoa said this, the tortoise opened its little beady black eyes and looked at my sister. Then it closed them and went to sleep again. So Mr Cocoa put it away in its box right at the back of the cupboard under the stairs.

'That's a funny animal,' my naughty little sister said.

After that, she talked and talked about the tortoise. She kept saying, 'When will it wake up? – When will it wake up?' But it didn't so she got tired of asking. By the time Christmas came she had almost forgotten it. And when the snow fell she quite forgot it.

And when spring came and the birds began to sing again, and she went in one day to have her morning cocoa with her next-door friend, Mrs Jones had forgotten it too!

They were just drinking their cocoa and Mrs Jones was telling my naughty little sister about some of the things she had done when she was a little girl when they heard:

Thump! Thump! Bang! Bang!

'Oh dear,' said Mrs Cocoa. 'There's some-one at the front door!' And she went to look. But there wasn't.

Thump! Thump!

'It must be the back door,' said Mrs Cocoa Jones, and she went to look but it wasn't!

Bang! Bang!

'What can it be?' asked Mrs Jones.

Now, my clever little sister had been listening hard. 'It's in the under-the-stairs place, Mrs Cocoa,' she said. 'Listen.'

Thump! Thump! Bang! Bang!

'Oh goodness,' said Mrs Cocoa. But she was a very brave lady. She opened the door of the cupboard and looked and my little sister looked too.

And Mrs Cocoa stared and my little sister stared.

There was the tortoise's wooden box, shaking and bumping because the cross tortoise inside had woken up and was banging to be let out.

'Goodness me,' said Mrs Cocoa. 'That tortoise has woken up!'

'Goodness me,' said my funny sister. 'That tortoise has woken up!'

And Mrs Cocoa looked hard at my sister and my sister looked hard at her.

'I shall have to see to it,' Mrs Cocoa said, and she picked up the bumping box and carried it into her kitchen and put the box on the table. Then she lifted my sister up to the chair so she could watch.

Mrs Cocoa lifted the lid off the box, and

there was that wide-awake tortoise. His head was waggle-waggling and his claws scratch-scratching to get out.

'I used to have a tortoise when I was a girl,' Mrs Cocoa said, 'so I know just what to do!'

And do you know what she did? She put some warm water into a bowl, and she put the tortoise in the warm water. Then she took it out and dried it very, very carefully on an old soft towel.

Then Mrs Cocoa put the clean fresh tortoise on the table, and said, 'Just mind it while I go and get it something to eat, there's a good child. Just put your hand gently on his back and he will stay quite still.'

My little sister did keep her hand on the tortoise's back and he was quite still until

Mrs Cocoa came back with a cabbage leaf.

'Look,' my naughty little sister said, 'look at his waggly head, Mrs Jones.'

And she put her face right down so she could see his little black eyes. 'Hello, Mister Tortoise,' she said.

And the tortoise made a funny noise at her. It said, 'His-ss-SS.'

My poor sister was surprised! She didn't like that noise very much. But Mrs Cocoa said the tortoise had only said, 'His-ss-SS' because it was hungry and not because it was cross. Mrs Cocoa said tortoises are nice friendly things so long as you let them go their own way.

And because my little sister had minded the tortoise for her she let her give him the cabbage leaf.

At first he only looked at it, and pushed it about with his beaky head, but at last he bit a big piece out of it.

'There!' Mrs Jones said. 'That's the first thing he's tasted since last summer!'

Just fancy that!

Mr Cocoa made the tortoise a little home in his rockery where it could sleep, and it could walk around among the stones or hide among the rockery flowers if it wanted to.

Sometimes it used to eat the flowers, and make Mr Cocoa cross.

That tortoise lived with the Cocoa Joneses for many, many years. It slept under the stairs in the winter and walked about the rockery in summer. It was still there when my sister was a grown-up lady.

Mr and Mrs Cocoa called it Henry, but of course when my sister was little she always called it Henry Cocoa Jones.

3 My Naughty Little Sister and Bad Harry at the library

Nowadays libraries are very nice places where there are plenty of picture-books for children to look at, and a very nice lady who will let you take some home to read so long as you promise not to tear them or scribble in them.

When I was a little girl we had a library in

the town where we lived. Our mother used to go there once a week to get a book to read, and when I was old enough I used to go with her to get a book for myself.

Our library wasn't as nice as the one nearest to your house. There wasn't a special children's part. The children's books were in a corner among the grown-up books, and all the books had dark brown library-covers – no nice bright picture-covers. You had to look inside them to find out what the stories were about.

Still, when I did look, I found some very good stories just as you do nowadays.

But we didn't have very nice people to give out the books.

There was a cross old man with glasses who didn't like children very much. When we brought our book back he would look through it very carefully to make sure we hadn't messed it up and grumble if he found a spot or a tear – even if it was nothing to do with us.

And there was a lady who used to say, 'Sh-sh-sh' all the time, and come and grumble if you held one book while you were looking at another one. She would say, 'All books to be returned to the shelves immediately.'

My little sister went to the library with us once, but she said she wouldn't come any more because she didn't like the shushy lady and the glasses man. So after that Mrs Cocoa Jones minded her on library days.

So, you can imagine how surprised we were one day when she said, 'I want to go the library.'

Our mother said, 'But you don't like the library. You're always saying how nasty it is there.'

But my little sister said, 'Yes, I do. I do like it *now*.'

She said, 'I don't want to go with you though, I want to go with Bad Harry's mother.'

What a surprise!

Our mother said, 'I don't suppose Harry's mother wants to take *you*. It must be hard enough for her with Harry.'

But, do you know, Harry's mother *did* want to take my sister. Bad Harry's mother said, '*Please* let her come with us. Harry has been worrying and worrying to ask you.'

So my mother said my little sister could go to the library with Bad Harry and his mother, but she said she thought she had better come along too.

'I don't trust those two bad children when they're together,' our mother said.

All the way to the library those naughty children walked in front of their mothers whispering and giggling together, and our mother said, 'I just hope they won't get up to mischief.'

But Harry's mother said, 'Oh no! *Harry is always as quiet as a mouse in the library*.'

Bad Harry – quiet as a mouse! Fancy that.

But so he was. And so was my sister. They were both as quiet as two mice.

When they got to the library, the man with glasses wasn't cross, he said, 'Hello, sonny,' to Bad Harry and that was a surprise. (But of course at that time Harry still looked good.)

And then the shushing lady came along. She smiled at Harry, and Harry smiled at her, and the lady looked at my naughty little sister and said, 'We don't mind good children like Harry coming here!'

My little sister was very surprised, and so was my mother, but Harry's mother said, 'Harry is always good in the library. He goes and sits in the little book-room in the corner, and he doesn't make a sound until I'm ready to go!'

Harry's mother said, 'He looks at the books on the table and he is as good as gold.'

Of course our mother was worried because she thought my sister couldn't be like that, but she let my sister go with Harry while she went to find herself a new book to read.

And, do you know, all the time our mother and Harry's mother were choosing books those children were quiet as mice.

And when our mother and Harry's mother were ready to go, there they were sitting good as gold, looking at a book in the little book-room.

When our mother got home she said, 'I would never have believed it. Those children were like *angels*!'

So after that my naughty little sister often went to the library with Bad Harry and his mother. And they were always quiet as mice.

Then one day Bad Harry's mother found out why.

One day when they were in the library she found a book very quickly, and, when she went along to the little book-room she had a great surprise. She couldn't see them anywhere!

Then she looked again, and there they were – under the book-table.

They were lying very still on their tummies, staring at something, and, as Harry's mother bent down to see what they were doing, a tiny mouse ran over the floor and into a hole in the wall!

You see, the very first time Harry had visited the library, he had seen that little mouse, and afterwards he always looked out for it.

He used to take things for it to eat sometimes: pieces of cheese and bacon-rind. The mouse had been Bad Harry's secret friend, and now it was my sister's secret friend too.

Harry's mother told our mother all about those funny children and the library mouse. She said, 'I suppose I ought to tell the librarian.'

But our mother said, 'I don't see why. That old man is always nibbling biscuits. He keeps them under the counter. He just encourages mice.'

I hadn't known about the biscuit nibbling, but the next time I went to get a book I peeped, and Mother was right. There was a bag of biscuits under the cross man's counter and *piles* of biscuit crumbs!

No wonder there was a library mouse.

And no wonder it made friends with Bad Harry. The cheese and bacon bits must have been a great change from biscuit crumbs, mustn't they?

4 Grandad's special holly

In the long time ago when I was a little girl with a naughty little sister, we had a dear old grandad who had two gardens. He had a pretty little garden round his house with flowers and apples in it, and a big garden near the park for vegetables. The garden near the park was called an allotment. It had a tall hedge at the bottom of it, and in this tall hedge was a big tree with green-and-white leaves. It was a very, very prickly tree.

We used to go and see Grandad when he

was working on his allotment. We used to take him something to drink because he said digging made him thirsty. In summer he had a jug of cold tea and in winter he had a jug of hot cocoa. In summer he would sit on his wheelbarrow and drink his tea and talk to us and in the wintertime we used to go into his allotment shed and warm our hands by the oil-stove while he drank his cocoa.

One day, when Grandad was drinking cold tea and the sun was shining, my little sister said, 'I don't like your prickly tree very much, Grandad. It prickled my fingers.'

Grandad said, 'That's a very special tree, that is. That's a variegated holly-tree. You don't see trees like that every day.' He said it in a very proud way.

He said, 'When Christmastime comes it

will be full of red berries.'

Then he told us that every Christmas Eve he would bring a ladder and climb up the holly-tree and cut off some of its beautiful green-and-white branches with the red berries. He would put the cut holly into his wheelbarrow and take it down to the Church.

Every Christmas Eve afternoon he took his holly to the Church so the church-ladies could hang it up on the walls and make them look nice for Christmas.

Grandad said, 'When I go to Church on Christmas Morning, I like to look up and see the greenery. I can always pick out my holly, it's special.'

When my little sister told our father about the holly he said he remembered how when he was a little boy he used to go with

Grandad to take the Church-holly on Christmas Eve. He said he could still remember going through the town with all the people pointing and saying, 'Look at the lovely holly!'

My little sister was pleased to hear about our father being a little boy and going to the Church with Grandad and the holly, and the next time we went to the allotment she told Grandad *she* would like to go with him on Christmas Eve.

And Grandad said well, if Mother didn't mind he'd be very pleased to take her when Christmas Eve came.

Our mother said she didn't mind a bit, because she knew Grandad would take great care of my sister. She said when Christmas Eve came if she still wanted to go with

Grandad it would be quite all right.

'Christmas Eve is a long way off,' our mother said. 'You may change your mind by then.'

But my naughty little sister *didn't* change her mind. Every time she saw Grandad she said, 'How are the holly-berries?' And when he showed her how they were growing and how red they were getting she got very impatient.

She kept saying, 'Will it soon be Christmas?' She was so afraid our dear old grandad would forget and take the holly without her.

But he didn't. On the very next Christmas Eve, just after we'd eaten our dinner there was a loud knock on the front-door, and when Mother opened it – there was

Grandad smiling and smiling and outside the gate was his great big wheel-barrow piled high with the lovely green-and-white and red-berried holly.

Some of the people in the road were looking out of their windows, and while our mother was putting my sister's warm coat on and tying the red woolly scarf round her neck, a lady came to our door and asked if Grandad would sell her some holly.

Grandad said, 'No, I'm very sorry, all this is for the Church.' But he gave the lady a little piece for her Christmas pudding and the lady was very glad to have it. My little sister said the lady's pudding would look very grand with special holly on it, and the lady said she was sure it would.

Now it was a long walk to the Church, so

our grandad said my little sister had better ride on the wheelbarrow. He had put some sacks in front of the barrow over the prickly leaves, and my little sister climbed on and sat down, and off they went.

My naughty little sister *did* enjoy that ride, even though the holly prickles poked through the sacks and scratched her a little bit. It was just like Father had said. All the people stared and said, 'What lovely holly!' and smiled at my little sister with her holly-berry red scarf sitting in front of Grandad's wheelbarrow.

They had to go down the High Street where the shops were because the Church was there too, and a man who sold oranges gave my sister one. He said, 'Happy Christmas, ducks,' to her as she went by. Wasn't

that nice of him? My sister thought it was and so did Grandad.

When they got to the Church the ladies all came out to look at Grandad's big load of variegated holly.

Grandad said, 'Lift it carefully, we don't want the berries knocked off.'

While Grandad and some of the ladies were taking the branches inside, one of the ladies talked to my little sister. She said, 'Would you like to come and see the manger?'

My little sister knew about 'Way in a Manger' and about Baby Jesus being born at Christmas time, so although she didn't know what the lady meant she said, 'Yes,' because she knew it would be something nice.

And so it was.

That kind lady took my little sister into the cold grey church where a lot of people were making it look bright and Christmassy with holly and ivy and white flowers in pots. My naughty little sister wanted to stop and look at a man on a ladder who was handing up some Christmas-tree branches, but the lady said, 'Come on.'

Then she said, 'There! It's just finished. Isn't it pretty?'

And there, in a corner of the cold old church someone had built a wooden shed with a manger with straw in it inside. There was a statue of Mary and a statue of Joseph standing on each side of the manger, and on the straw inside it was a little stony Baby Jesus statue.

There was a picture of an ox and a

donkey on the wall at the back of the shed, and round the shed doorway were pictures of angels.

My little sister said, 'My grandad's got a shed like that on his allotment. He's got a stove in it though.'

And she looked very hard at the Mary statue and the Joseph statue and the Baby Jesus statue.

The lady said, 'The Sunday School children always bring toys to Church on Christmas Day to send to the children in hospital. They leave them by the manger because that's where the shepherds put their presents.' The lady said that tomorrow morning there would be some shepherd statues by the manger too.

Then she said, 'You can stay and look if

you like. I'll just go and help your grandaddy
to break up some of the holly branches.'

So my naughty little sister stayed there,
looking and looking. It was very cold in that

big church. Mary looked cold and Joseph looked cold too. Very, very carefully my little sister leaned into the shed and touched the little Baby Jesus statue and he was cold as ice!

My naughty little sister stayed by the manger for a little while longer and then she went to find Grandad who was ready to go home. There was lots of room in the wheelbarrow now, and lots more things to see on the way home, but my little sister was very, very quiet.

And what do you think happened?

The next day, which was Christmas Day of course, when I went with the other Sunday School boys and girls to leave a present by the manger for the ill children, we saw a very strange thing.

There were Mary and Joseph. The Shepherds were there too. And there was the little Baby Jesus!

But the little Baby Jesus wasn't cold any more. He was wrapped up in my naughty little sister's red woolly scarf, and he had an orange beside him!

The Sunday School teacher said, 'Your funny little sister did that last night! Wasn't that sweet of her? She thought he was cold!'

5 Granny's wash-day

Long ago, when I was a little girl with a naughty little sister we had two grannies. We had a granny who lived near us and a granny in the country.

We could see our near-granny whenever we wanted to, but we only saw our country-granny when we could go and stay with her.

Our country-granny lived in a pretty house with roses all over it. It was a funny house. One of the funny things about it was that there were no taps in it at all.

There was a big pump in the back garden. This pump was on top of a deep well full of clear cold water. Our granny got all her water out of that well.

One time my naughty little sister went to stay with this granny and she liked it very much. There were five kind uncles living there too and they made a great fuss of my little sister.

But although these uncles were so kind they made such a lot of noise and needed such a lot of looking-after and ate such very big dinners that my little sister said, 'I shan't have any boys when I'm a lady.'

Every day our granny cooked big dinners for all the hungry uncles. Every day our hungry uncles ate all the big dinners up. On *Sunday* Granny cooked such a *big, big* dinner that my little sister said, 'Do the uncles eat more than ever because it's Sunday?'

'Oh, no, my dear,' our granny said. 'I always cook extra potatoes and extra cabbage for *bubble-and-squeak*. Tomorrow is wash-day,' Granny said. 'I don't have time for much cooking on wash-day.'

When Granny said 'bubble-and-squeak' my little sister laughed. She hadn't heard about bubble-and-squeak before. So she said it lots of times. She said, 'Bubble-and-squeak, bubble-and-squeak,' over and over again. It sounded so bubbly and so squeaky when she said it to herself that she could hardly stop laughing at all.

When my little sister *did* stop laughing she asked what 'bubble-and-squeak' was. But our granny said, 'Wait until tomorrow and then you can taste some.'

(Do you know what bubble-and-squeak is? If you don't you'll know at the end of the story.)

Well, next day was Monday and Monday was wash-day at our granny's house.

Our granny's wash-day was a very busy day. Everyone got up very, very early. Even my little sister. She heard all the people moving about and she got up to see what they were doing.

Our uncles carried lots of large pails out to the garden, and pumped up water and filled all the pails up to the top. Then those kind men carried all the heavy pails back to the house and left them by the back door. They wanted to help their mother so they fetched all the water for wash-day before they had their breakfasts.

When our uncles had gone off to work my little sister helped Granny too. She helped Granny collect all the dirty things that had to be washed.

My little sister liked helping to do this. It was great fun. Granny took all the sheets and pillow-cases off the beds and all the towels and our uncles' dirty shirts and things and she put them outside the bedroom doors. Then my little sister took all the sheets and pillow-cases and towels and all the other things from outside the bedroom doors and *she threw them all down the stairs*. And she wasn't being naughty. She threw them down the stairs because Granny said it saved carrying them down.

It was very nice throwing the dirty things

down the stairs and my little sister was sorry when there was nothing left to throw. But she was a good child. She went downstairs with Granny and helped her to carry the things out to the wash-house next to the back-door.

Do you know what a wash-house is? I will tell you what our granny's wash-house was like. It was a long room. In a corner there was a big copper for boiling the water. There was a fire burning under the copper to make the water hot. There was a big sink and lots of big baths full of cold water for rinsing the washing.

Granny had a big wringer for wringing the wet clothes in her wash-house. She had some clothes lines too. She had them hanging up in the wash-house in case it

rained on wash-day.

A lady called Mrs Apple came to help Granny do her washing. She had a brown apron on with a big pocket in front of it, and this big pocket was full of pegs.

My little sister had never seen such a big wash-day before. She was so interested she got in Granny's way. She got in Mrs Apple's way too. Mrs Apple dipped a funny little bag full of blue stuff into one of the baths full of water and made the water blue, and my naughty little sister liked it so much she splashed and dabbled in it and got herself wet.

Granny said, 'Oh dear, you're as bad as your mother used to be on wash-days when she was your age.'

My sister was surprised to hear that our mother had been a naughty little girl when she was little.

Kind Mrs Apple said, 'Ah, but your mummy was a good girl too. Now, see if you can be a good girl.' And she gave my little sister a basin full of warm water and let her wash her own cotton socks and handkerchiefs. Mrs Apple said, 'It will be a great help if you do those.'

So my little sister rubbed and rubbed and when they were as clean as they could be, kind Mrs Apple let her put them into the big copper for boiling.

She held my little sister up so that she could drop the socks and handkerchiefs in for herself. Then Mrs Apple put more wood on the copper fire and said, 'They will all cook nicely now.'

Then Mrs Apple washed and washed and

our granny rinsed and rinsed. The wringer was turned and the water ran out of the clothes. The copper steamed and steamed and my little sister was so interested and got in the way so much that at last our granny said, 'I know what I will do with you. I will do the same thing I used to do to your mother and your uncles when they got in the way on wash-days.'

What do you think that was? It was something very nice. Our granny went to a shelf and took down a little chair-swing with strong ropes on it. Then she climbed up on a chair and my little sister saw that there were two big hooks in the wash-house roof. Granny put the ropes over the hooks. She tried the swing with her hands to make sure it was safe and strong and then she lifted my naughty little sister into the swing and gave it a big push.

My little sister had a lovely time swinging in the steamy splashy wash-house. Now she was not in the way at all and she could see everything that was happening.

Sometimes Granny gave her a little push.

Sometimes Mrs Apple pushed. Sometimes my little sister swung herself.

My little sister sang and sang and Mrs Apple said it was nice to hear her. She said my little sister sounded just like a dickey-bird.

When the washing was quite finished, Granny lifted my little sister out of the swing, and then Granny and Mrs Apple and my little sister all had cups of cocoa and bread-and-cheese. My little sister was very hungry because she had got up so early. Granny and Mrs Apple were hungry because they had worked so hard.

After that they all went into the garden where there were more clothes-lines, and my little sister held the peg basket for Granny while she pegged out the sheets.

Mrs Apple had pegs in her pocket so she didn't have to hold out the basket for her.

There were three long clothes-lines in Granny's garden and when the sheets and towels and shirts and things were blowing in the wind my sister saw what a lot of washing they had done. She was very glad to see the socks and handkerchiefs she had washed blowing too.

Then Mrs Apple went off to her own house to get her husband's dinner.

'*Now*,' said Granny, 'I shall cook that bubble-and-squeak. Come and watch me and then when you grow up you will know how to make it for yourself.'

First Granny put a lot of meaty-looking dripping into a big black frying-pan. She put the pan on top of the stove. The fat got very hot, and when it was hot it was all runny and bubbly. Then Granny took the cold potatoes and the cold cabbage that she had cooked on Sunday, and she put them all into the pan.

Granny cooked the potatoes and the cabbage in the hot fat until they were a lovely goldy-brown colour.

'The bubble-and-squeak is finished now,' Granny said, and she put it on a hot plate and popped it into the oven to keep warm, until our uncles came home for dinner.

It was very nice indeed! My naughty little sister said so and so did our hungry uncles. My little sister ate and ate and the uncles ate and ate.

My little sister said, 'Can I have some more bubble-and-squeak, please?' when she had finished her first lot.

'Why, you eat more than we do,' our uncles said.

'Yes,' said my naughty little sister, 'but I have been working hard today and it's made me very hungry.'

She said, 'I think bubble-and-squeak is the best wash-day dinner in the world.'

6 Crusts

A long time ago, when my sister was a little girl, she didn't like eating bread-and-butter crusts.

Our mother was very cross about this, because she had to eat crusts when she was a little girl, and she thought my sister should eat her crusts up too!

Every day at tea-time, Mother would put a piece of bread-and-butter on our plates and say, '*Plain* first. *Jam* second, and *cake if you're lucky!*'

She would say '*Plain* first. *Jam* second, and *cake if you're lucky*,' because that is what our granny used to say to her when she was a little girl.

That meant that we ought to eat plain bread-and-butter before we had some with jam on, and all the bread – even the crusts – or we wouldn't get any cake.

I always ate my piece of bread-and-butter up straight away like a good girl, but my naughty little sister didn't. She used to bend her piece in half and nibble out the middle soft part and leave the crust on her plate.

Sometimes she played games with the crust – she would hold it up and peep through the hole and say, 'I see you.'

Sometimes she would put her hand through it and say, 'I've got a wrist-watch!' And sometimes she would break it up into little pieces and leave them all over the table cloth. But she never, never ate it. Wasn't she a wasteful child?

Then, when she'd stopped playing with her bread-and-butter crust my bad little sister would say, 'Cake.'

'Cake,' she would say. 'Cake – *please*.'

Our mother would say, 'What about that crust? Aren't you going to eat it?'

And my naughty little sister would shake her head. 'All messy. Nasty crust,' she would say.

'No crust. No cake,' Mother said. But it didn't make any difference though. My bad sister said, 'I'll get down then!' And if anyone tried to make her eat her crust she would scream and scream.

Our mother didn't know what to do. She told Mrs next-door Cocoa Jones and Mrs Cocoa said, 'Try putting something nice on the crusts. See if she will eat them then!'

Mrs Cocoa said, 'She loves pink fish-paste, try that.'

So next day at tea-time our mother said, 'Will you eat your crusts up if I put pink fish-paste on them?'

And my naughty little sister said, 'Oh, *pink* fish-paste!' because that was a very great treat. 'I like pink fish-paste,' my sister said.

So our mother put some pink fish-paste on the crust that my little sister had left.

'*Now* eat it up,' Mother said.

But my sister didn't eat her crust after all. No. Do you know what she did? She licked all the fish-paste off her crust and then she put it back on her plate and said, 'Finished. No cake. Get down now.'

Wasn't she a naughty girl?

One day during the time when my sister wouldn't eat crusts Bad Harry and his mother came to tea at our house.

When Bad Harry's mother saw that my

little sister wasn't eating her crusts she was very surprised. She said, 'Why aren't you eating your crusts?'

My sister said, 'I don't like them.'

Bad Harry's mother said, 'But you always eat your crusts when you come to our house. You eat them all up then, just like Harry does.'

We were amazed when we heard Bad Harry's mother say that. She said, 'They don't leave crust or crumb!' But my naughty little sister didn't say anything and Bad Harry didn't say anything either.

When our father came home from work and Mother told him about my sister eating her crusts at Harry's house, Father was very stern.

'That shows you've got to be firm with that child,' he said, and he shook his finger at my sister.

'No more crusts left on plates. I *mean* it.' He did look cross.

And my naughty little sister said in a tiny little voice. 'No crusts like Harry? No crusts like Bad Harry.'

And Father said, 'No crusts like Good Harry.

No crusts or *I will know the reason why*.'

So after that there were no more crusts on my little sister's plate and she ate cake after that like everyone else.

But one day, a long time afterwards when our mother was spring-cleaning, she was dusting under the table, and saw some funny green mossy-stuff growing out from a crack underneath the table-top.

This crack belonged to a little drawer that had lost its handle and hadn't been opened for a long time.

Mother said, 'Goodness. What on earth is that?' And she went and fetched something to hook into the drawer, and then she tried to pull it out. It took a long time because the drawer was stuck.

Mother pulled and prodded and tapped

and all of a sudden the drawer rushed out so quickly it fell on to the floor.

And all over the floor was a pile of green mouldy crusts!

My naughty little sister had found that crack under the table and pushed all her crusts into the drawer when no one was looking!

My sister was very surprised to see all that mossy-looking old bread. She had forgotten all about it.

When Mother scolded her she said, 'I must have been very naughty. I eat my crusts now though, don't I?'

'And we thought you were being good like Harry,' our mother said, and then my sister laughed and laughed.

And do you want to know why she did

that? Well, a long time after that, Harry's father got the gas-men to put a new stove in their kitchen, and when the gas-men took the old gas-cooker out they found lots and lots of old dried-up crusts behind it.

When our mother heard about this, she laughed too. 'Fancy us expecting you to learn anything *good* from that Bad Harry,' she said.

7 My Naughty Little Sister and the ring

A long time ago, when I was a little girl and my sister was a very, very little girl she was always putting things into her mouth to see what they tasted like.

Even things that weren't meant to be tasted. And even though our mother had told her over and over again that it was a naughty thing to do.

Our mother would say, 'Look at that

child! She's got something in her mouth *again*!'

She would pick my sister up and say, 'Now, now, Baby, give it to Mother.'

And my naughty little sister would take it out of her mouth and put it into Mother's hand.

My sister tasted all sorts of silly things; pennies, pencils, nails, pebbles – things like that.

Our mother said, 'One day you will swallow something like this, and then you *will* have a tummy-ache!'

But do you know, even though my sister didn't want to have a tummy-ache she *still* put things in her mouth!

Our mother said, 'It is a very bad habit.'

Well now, one day, a lady called Mrs

Clarke came to tea with us. Mrs Clarke was very fond of children, and when she saw my little sister all neat and tidied up for the visit, she said, 'What a dear little girl.'

Now, my little sister was quite a shy child, and sometimes when people came to our house she would hide behind our mother's skirt. But when Mrs Clarke said she was a dear little girl, and when she saw what a nice lady Mrs Clarke was, she smiled at her at once and went and sat on her lap when she asked her to.

Mrs Clarke played 'Ride a cock horse' with my little sister. Then she took my sister's fat little hand and played 'Round and round the garden' on it. Then she told my sister a funny little poem and made her laugh. My naughty little sister *did* like Mrs Clarke.

She liked her so much that when Mrs Clarke and our mother started talking to each other, she stayed on Mrs Clarke's lap and was as good as gold.

First my sister looked up at Mrs Clarke's nice powdery face. Then she twisted round and looked at the pretty flowers on Mrs Clarke's dress. There were some sparkly buttons on Mrs Clarke's dress too.

My sister touched all those sparkly buttons to see if they were hard or soft and then she turned again and looked at Mrs Clarke's hands.

When Mrs Clarke talked she waved and waved her hands, and my naughty little sister saw there was something very sparkly indeed on one of Mrs Clarke's fingers.

My sister said, 'Button. Pretty button,'

and tried to get hold of it.

Our mother said, 'Why, she thinks it's one of your buttons!'

Mrs Clarke said, 'It's a ring dear. It's my diamond ring. Would you like to see it?' and she took the ring off her finger so that my little sister could hold it.

The diamond ring was very, very sparkly indeed. My little sister turned it and turned it, and lots of shiny lights came out of it in all directions. Sometimes the lights were white and sometimes they had colours in them. My sister couldn't stop looking at it.

Mrs Clarke said my sister could mind her ring for a little while, and then she and Mother started talking again.

Presently my little sister began to wonder if the ring would taste as sparkly as it looked. It was sparklier than fizzy lemonade. So of course she put the ring in her mouth, and of course it didn't taste like lemonade at all.

After that my sister listened to Mother and Mrs Clarke talking.

Mrs Clarke was a funny lady and she said things that made our mother laugh, and although my sister didn't know what she was laughing about, my sister began to laugh too, and Mrs Clarke hugged her and said she was a 'funny little duck'.

It was very nice until Mrs Clarke said, 'Well, I must think about going home soon,' because then she said, 'I'll have to have my ring back now, lovey.'

And the ring wasn't there.

It wasn't in my sister's hand. It wasn't on the table, or on the floor. *And it wasn't in my sister's mouth either.*

Our mother said, 'Did you put it in your mouth?' and she looked at my sister very hard.

And my sister said, in a tiny, tiny voice, 'Yes.'

Then our mother said, 'She must have swallowed it.' Mother looked so worried when she said this, that my sister got very frightened and began to scream.

She remembered what Mother had said about swallowing things that weren't meant to be eaten. She said, 'Oh! Oh! Tummy-ache! Tummy-ache!'

But Mrs Clarke said, 'It wouldn't be in your tummy yet, you know.' The sensible lady said, 'We'll take you along to the doctor's.'

But my sister went on crying and shouting, 'Swallowed it. Swallowed it.'

No one could stop her.

Then Father came home. When he heard the noise he was quite astonished. He shouted, 'Quiet, quiet,' to my sister in such a

bellowy voice that she stopped at once.

Then Father said, 'What's all the fuss about?' and our mother told him.

Father looked at my little sister, and then he looked at Mrs Clarke. He stared very hard at Mrs Clarke and then he laughed and laughed.

'Look,' he said, 'Look – look at Mrs Clarke's button.'

Mrs Clarke looked, Mother looked and even my frightened little sister looked, and there was the ring hanging on one of Mrs Clarke's shiny buttons!

My silly little sister had taken it out of her mouth and hung it on to one of Mrs Clarke's dress-buttons to see which was the most glittery, and then she had forgotten all about it.

When our mother had said she must have swallowed it, my sister really thought she had.

She'd even thought she had a tummy-ache.

And she'd screamed and made a fuss.

What a silly child.

Father and Mother and Mrs Clarke laughed and laughed and laughed – they were so glad my naughty little sister hadn't swallowed the ring after all!

My sister didn't laugh though, she hid her face in Mother's lap and wouldn't come out again until Mrs Clarke had gone home.

But she never put anything in her mouth again – except the right things of course, like food and sweeties, and *toothbrushes*!

8 Harry's very bad day

When my naughty little sister's friend Harry was a very little boy he was often bad without knowing it. I expect you used to be like that sometimes.

Once Harry had a day being bad like that.

One day, when his mother was busy cleaning her house and his father was busy sawing wood in the garden Harry climbed up on to a chair in the kitchen and began to bang a spoon on a plate.

Harry sometimes banged his spoon on the

plate after he had eaten his dinner and nobody had grumbled at him. But Harry's dinner-plate was the sort that doesn't break.

This day Harry banged a spoon on one of his mother's best china dinner-plates. It made a much nicer noise than Harry's own plate did so he hit it harder and harder. Presently

he hit it on the edge, and it jumped and fell off the table on to the hard kitchen floor.

And of course it broke.

Bad Harry said, 'Broke!' in a very surprised voice.

Then he said, 'Broke it. Broke it all up.'

'*Broke it*,' he shouted and his mother heard him and came and grumbled at him.

'Oh Harry, you are a bad, bad boy,' she said. 'I can't take my eyes off you for one minute.'

Harry said, 'Plate broke. All fall down.'

'Yes, and *you* broke it,' said Harry's mother. 'It was very, very naughty.'

She said, 'I can't watch you all the time. You had better go out in the garden and watch Daddy. He is making me some new shelves.'

So Bad Harry took his spoon and went out into the garden to see what his father was doing.

'Stand there if you want to watch,' Harry's father said. 'Don't come any nearer or you might get sawn by mistake, and you wouldn't like that.'

So Bad Harry stood still and watched.

Harry's father had a plank of wood on his bench and he was sawing.

Zzzz-zzz, Zzzz-zzz went the saw, and all the yellow sawdust fell on to the ground.

Zzzz-zzz, Zzzz-zzz, Zzzz-zzz went the bright shining saw, and then, *plunk!* a piece of wood fell off.

'Another shelf cut,' Harry's father said, and he took it indoors to measure it against the kitchen wall. He took the saw too. He didn't want Harry to play with that.

But Harry didn't want to play with the saw anyway. He wanted to play with the heap of yellow sawdust.

First he put his foot in it, and pushed it round and made it all swirly.

Then he knelt down and put his spoon in it. He tried to taste it, but it was nasty and stuck to his tongue, so he spat it out again. Then he threw spoonfuls of sawdust up in the air. It blew all over the flowerbed. 'There it goes,' Harry said.

'There it goes,' and he threw some more. He liked doing that.

Presently, he dropped his spoon and picked up two big, big handfuls of sawdust and threw it up in the air at once, but it didn't blow away – it all came down on his head! It got all mixed up in his curls.

But Harry didn't mind. He threw up some more sawdust and began to laugh.

'Up in the air,' he said. 'Up in the air.'

He thought it was a very nice game.

Harry's father was very cross when he came out and saw the mess on his flower-beds; he didn't think it was a nice game; he shouted at Harry.

Harry's mother was very cross when she saw all the sawdust in Harry's hair. She had to brush it out at once.

'I suppose you'd better come with *me*,' Harry's mother said and she took him upstairs with her, and sat him on the floor and found him some toys to play with. 'Now behave yourself,' she said, and went back to polish the floor again.

But Bad Harry didn't like those toys very much – he didn't want to play with them at all. He wanted to help his mother do her work.

So he went across the room and he found a big tin full of yellow polish, and while his mother was polishing the floor he rubbed it all over the chairs, and the dressing-table. He took it out of the tin with his hands and he rubbed it everywhere.

He liked doing that. He said, 'Look, I polish.'

Harry's mother looked and she was so cross she shouted, '*Harry*!' – like that. '*Harry*! I've had quite enough of you for one day. You shall go straight to bed.'

And she washed all the polish off him, and put him into his pyjamas and then she put him to bed. 'Stay there you bad, bad boy,' she said. '*Don't you dare to get up.*'

Harry was very cross with his mother for putting him to bed like that. He didn't think he'd been naughty. So he got out of bed and screamed and banged and shouted till his father called out, 'Do you want me to come up there?' and then he was very quiet.

He was so quiet his mother nearly forgot all about him. When she did remember him again she went in to see what he was doing. When she saw him she began to laugh.

Bad Harry had forgotten all about being sent to bed because he was naughty. He had kicked his legs up in the air under the bedclothes and made a little tent, and taken his Teddy and all his toys into the tent with him.

'I've made a house,' Harry said.

And he wouldn't go downstairs. He liked playing house so much he stayed on his bed all the afternoon, laughing and talking to himself.

My mother brought us round to see Harry's mother that afternoon and when my little sister heard him laughing upstairs she ran up to see what he was doing.

She liked his game so much, she went into the little house too and they had a lovely time.

'I put him to bed for being naughty,' Harry's mother said. 'I think I shall have to put him there when I want him to be good.'

9 Bad Harry and Mrs Cocoa's art-pot

Long ago, when Bad Harry was very small, he had beautiful golden curls and looked very good. Afterwards he had a haircut and then he looked as naughty as my sister did.

Well now, here is a story about the time before Harry had his hair cut.

One day, all the people where we lived were very excited because a famous lady was coming to our town.

Bad Harry's father was specially excited because he was one of the people who had asked this lady to come. Lots of people came to his house to talk about the lady's visit, and say what they ought to do to make things nice for her.

She was going to make a speech in the parish hall, and Harry's father said they must put lots of flowers in the hall to make it look pretty. He went round asking people if they would lend vases to put flowers in, and if they could spare some flowers from their gardens to go in the vases.

Our mother said she would lend some vases, and Father said he would send some of his flowers. Mrs Cocoa Jones who lived next door to us, said she didn't think Mr Jones would like to cut his flowers, but she would lend her fern in the brass art-pot.

That was very kind of Mrs Cocoa because that fern in the brass art-pot was in her sitting-room window and she liked to see it there when she came up her front path every day.

Lots of people promised to find some flowers for the hall. One lady said she thought someone ought to give the famous lady some flowers for herself. She said, 'I think Harry should do it. With all those lovely curls he would be sweet.'

Harry's father wasn't very sure about this, but the lady said, 'Oh yes, after all he is your little boy – and you have worked so hard.'

Bad Harry's father said, 'Well, I'll ask him, but I don't think he'll want to do it.'

But Harry *did* want to do it. He wanted to

do it very much.

So his father took him down to the parish hall and he practised walking up the steps on one side of the platform, and bowing and pretending to give the flowers to the lady and going off on the other side of the platform, and he did it beautifully.

He practised so hard that when the Lady's Visit Day came he did it perfectly. He walked up on to the platform, and bowed and gave the lady the flowers and looked so good and nice that everyone in the hall smiled and clapped and the actress lady gave him a kiss.

He was Good Harry then – but oh dear!

After Harry had given the lady her flowers he had to go and sit down in the front row of the hall with his mother, because his father and the other people who'd asked the lady to come were staying up on the platform with her. So, when Harry got down his mother was waiting to take him to his seat.

Now all the seats in the hall had pieces of paper on them. They had been put there for people to read. When Bad Harry got to his seat there was a piece of paper for him too. Bad Harry picked up his piece of paper and pretended to read it like the grown-up people were doing, but he soon got tired of that and started to look around and fidget.

The people on the platform began to talk. Then Harry's father said something, and people clapped, and then the lady began to speak. Harry listened for a little while but he didn't understand what she was talking about, so he began to flap his piece of paper.

Then he pretended it was an aeroplane and moved it about in the air over his head.

Harry's mother got very cross. She snatched his piece of paper away from him and said, 'Behave yourself.'

She snatched so hard she left a little piece of the paper in Harry's hand!

Poor Harry! He was *trying* to be good. Now he tried very hard indeed. He sat very still and stared straight in front of him.

And there – right in front of him on the platform – was Mrs Cocoa's lovely shiny brass pot with the fern in it standing among the other ferns and vases of flowers.

Harry looked hard at Mrs Cocoa's pot – and, in its shiny brass side, he saw a funny little boy looking at him. It was himself of course.

Have you ever seen those mirrors that make you look all sorts of funny shapes – they have them at fairs sometimes? Well, that's the sort of funny shape Harry-in-the-pot looked like.

Harry was very interested to see himself looking like that. He put his head forward – and the boy in the pot looked like an upside-down pear with big curls on top!

Then he stuck his chin up and that made his eyes look wavy. He turned his head this way, and that way – and every time he moved Harry-in-the-pot looked stranger and stranger.

It was a lovely game. Harry began to pull faces and the faces in Mrs Cocoa's pot were uglier than the ones Harry made!

And then: do you remember the little piece of paper Harry still had in his hand? Can you guess what he did with it?

He licked the piece of paper, and stuck it on his nose!

And then he pulled such a dreadful face

at himself, and Harry-in-the-pot with a piece of paper on his nose pulled such a funny face back at him that he laughed out loud.

Now all the people sitting up on the platform had been looking at the lady and listening to her talking, but soon first one and then another looked down and saw Bad Harry making those dreadful faces. They began to look very shocked, especially as Bad Harry's mother was looking up at the lady and hadn't noticed what he was doing.

She didn't look at Harry until he laughed out loud. Then she looked – and so did the Famous Lady.

Harry's mother was very cross indeed, but the lady wasn't. When she saw Bad Harry with the piece of paper stuck on his nose making dreadful faces and laughing she stopped talking and began to laugh too.

She laughed so much, all the people in the parish hall laughed as well, though at first they didn't know what she was laughing at.

Harry's mother didn't laugh though. She was very cross. She picked Harry up quickly and hurried down the hall with him and then the people laughed more than ever because he had still got the piece of paper stuck on his nose!

The lady wasn't a bit cross. Later on she told Harry's father she hadn't enjoyed herself so much for ages.

Now our mother was at that meeting, and she told us about it afterwards. She was quite shocked.

But my naughty little sister wasn't shocked. She was very interested. And do you know what she did?

As soon as Mrs Cocoa's shining brass pot was back in her sitting-room window she went straight round to have a look at it for herself, and she pulled faces at herself and made herself laugh, like Bad Harry had done!

And after that, when Bad Harry came to play at our house, they sometimes asked Mrs Cocoa if they could come and play 'Funny Faces' with her art-pot, and if she had got time, and their shoes weren't muddy, kind Mrs Cocoa would let them!